The Questions Within

TERESA SCHAEFFER

Ransom

The Questions Within

TERESA SCHAEFFER

Series Editor: Peter Lancett

Published by Ransom Publishing Ltd.
51 Southgate Street, Winchester, Hampshire SO23 9EH, UK
www.ransom.co.uk

ISBN 978 184167 700 2

First published in 2008
Copyright © 2008 Ransom Publishing Ltd.
Cover by Flame Design, Cape Town, South Africa

Born in Baltimore, Maryland, Teresa Schaeffer grew up with foster-care children through much of her childhood. This difficult beginning has given her a sensitivity and insight that is expressed through her work as a novelist, poet, filmmaker and screenwriter.

Teresa has also written two books of poetry, *The Birth of a Rose* and *The Burning Sand*, both of which have been published.

IN THE SAME SERIES

CHAPTER 1

Today started off like any other day. I awoke to my alarm clock obnoxiously blaring in my ear at precisely 6:25 am. Sometimes that alarm can start me off in a bad mood because I really don't want to get up, but today I am consumed by a sense of complete bliss.

Anyhow, where was I? Oh yes, my day. Well, I took my shower, put on some make-up and slipped into my freshly pressed khaki shorts and polo shirt. I just had my hair done the other day and it is fabulous. It is pretty short, just above my chin, perfectly styled. I'd like to think I look nice, but other people may think differently.

This morning is the first day of my last year in high school. I am excited, yet I feel strangely nervous too. Still, I am determined to walk through those black metal doors with a smile on my face. In my mind, today is a new beginning, the first day of the rest of my life. I can at last hold my head up high – I think. I hope.

The last ten years of my life have been a little rough. It has been a long road, but I am so glad that I am past those times and that I actually made it. I now have an imaginary umbrella every day of my life to shield me from the rain that occasionally pours.

Isn't it funny that when you were a young child everything was such fun and so easy? When I was about five years old I loved to play outside with my friends. My neighbour had a fake kind of amusement park at her house every weekend. My friend Lily and I would go over there and have so much fun, riding down the steps on a blanket or sitting in the middle of a huge parachute, being thrown up into the air. Those are a few good memories that I have.

Lily was my age and we were such good friends. We sat on the bus next to each other on our first day of infants and the few years that followed. We were practically inseparable, even though we were very different from one another.

She was the type of girl to play with Barbie dolls and play dress-up in her mom's clothing. Me on the other hand, I hated Barbie dolls and only played with them when she forced me to. I always fancied Lego or GI Joe and *only* played dress-up with my dad's ties or hats. She would always look at me curiously, wondering why I hated dresses, wore high-top sneakers and loved to get dirty. But she loved me anyway... until third grade came along...

Wow, it's ten past seven already. I've been going on and on, almost forgetting that I have to be in class in an hour. I have to put my shoes on, and then I will be ready to go. Man, I love these shoes; classic Adidas. They are simple, black and white, and extremely clean. I have a tendency to wash them every day. I can not handle even a speck of dirt on them. Obsessive? A little, but I have always been this way. I love nice clothes. No one should wear dirty shoes with fresh and clean gear. That just isn't right at all!

Speaking of which, that brings me back to my third grade year, the second day of school to be exact. I remember that day like it was yesterday. In the first three years of school I hadn't made many friends. Lily was pretty much still the only friend I had. For some reason no one talked to me; they just gave me dirty looks, like I had some contagious disease or something.

Well, that day was a day that changed my whole outlook on myself and my life. It is when I started to think that I was really weird and disgusting.

Lily was acting strange with me that day, barely talking to me or looking at me. I tried to act like nothing was going on but when break came, I got a slap in the face.

The entire class was going outside to play, practically running. I walked over to Lily.

'Hey! You okay?" I asked.

She gave me a really odd look.

'Uh yeah, why?'

Right there and then I knew something was wrong, because she wasn't even looking at me. She was just looking around the classroom at the other kids leaving, and the two snobby girls at the door who were waiting for her.

'I dunno, you've been acting weird to me all week,' I said.

'Well... I just think we can't be friends anymore.'

'What? What are you talkin' about?'

'You are kinda odd; always dressing like a boy and well... you just *are* weird. Sorry.'

She said it without even blinking or betraying any emotion at all.

I stood there not saying anything and she walked away towards her new friends at the doorway. I felt the tears coming fast, my eyes full, but I pushed them back; after all I didn't want to appear to be a baby. I looked down at my long shorts and took off the baseball cap that I was wearing. I never thought that it was weird that I loved boys clothing or never cared about boys like the other girls did. But Lily had told me straight.

I lost my best friend in that moment and I was suddenly alone, with no one to talk to at all, and I knew it. I remember walking outside to the basketball hoops at break by myself, just standing there by myself.

A couple of boys were playing basketball and their ball bounced towards me. This kid named Chris walked over to grab the ball that had stopped by my feet.

'Aren't ya going to give it to me?'

I didn't say anything, just picked up the ball and handed it to him. He took it from me, standing there briefly and sort of staring.

'Thanks, ugly.'

Then he just ran back to the three other boys he was playing ball with. They all turned and looked at me, laughing.

I stood there and watched them for a minute or so, then walked back towards the school doors. I wanted to go home and stay there; I didn't want to be at school or around anyone. I just wanted to crawl into a little ball and hide. I didn't have anyone to talk to anymore, not even Lily.

That then, was the day when my life changed alright and the years that followed were like a roller coaster ride.

Today, so many memories are brought to the surface. But not in a bad way though, because my memories just serve to show me how far I have come.

I'd better get downstairs. I know my mom has probably made me some breakfast which I will have to wolf down so that I can get going. It takes me about 15 minutes to walk to school. I don't know why my mom makes me walk because the school is a mile away, but I guess it is good exercise.

Oh yeah, I can't forget my book bag. All this nostalgia has distracted me. I love my book bag; it is black and actually it's a sort of messenger bag. It is covered with metal badges. I have a few that are the rainbow flag and a few others with funny quotes. Actually, I have never gone to school with them pinned on my bag before, but like I said, today is different; a new day.

CHAPTER 2

Walking down the stairs to the kitchen I can smell breakfast. My mom has gone all out this morning for breakfast. She's made omelettes, bacon and toast. This is way out of the ordinary; normally I eat cereal of some sort. I really have no idea what has gotten into her lately. She seems to be doing a lot for me, much more than usual even.

In the kitchen I see my mom in her dressing gown sitting at the table reading the newspaper. She smiles over at me.

'Good morning, sweetie.'

She lays the newspaper down on the table, stands up and goes over to the stove.

'Hi, Mom. A lot of food this morning, huh?'

'Yeah, but it's your first day back to school. It's a big day for you. Are you excited?'

Mom grabs a plate from the cabinet next to the stove and loads it with food.

'I guess so. I'm just glad I am almost finished.'

She hands me the plate, smiling.

'You look nice.'

I look down at my outfit, like I'm inspecting myself.

'Thanks,' I say to her.

I take the plate over to the table. I can't believe how much food is on there; I really don't know how I am going to eat it all.

I take a bite as my mom sits down at the table across from me.

'Good food, Mom.'

She just smiles, then picks up the newspaper and starts to read it again.

I love my mom dearly, but we have had some difficult times. Even now it is hard to believe everything she says to me. She tells me that she thinks I look nice, but in the back of her mind she is probably wishing I was like a *normal* girl, wearing girly clothing and even walking more like a lady.

I do have this certain strut, and no matter how hard I try I cannot change it. I've walked this way since I was a little kid. Maybe it started because I felt like I had to act tough, let people know not to mess with me. I don't know, but the strut is still with me and all I can say is that I am who I am, like it or not.

When I was about twelve or so, my mom started to try to make me wear clothes that

I didn't want to wear. I'd walk into my room after school some days to find an outfit on my bed, nice fitting and girlie, rather than the boys' clothing a couple sizes too big that I preferred. I remember getting so upset with my mom on those days, and asking her why she kept on picking out stuff for me that I would never wear. Inside I'd be hurt because I felt like she was embarrassed and ashamed to have me as a daughter.

The thing was, she was okay with me being a tomboy as a young kid. Lots of other kids were like that too. It only became a big deal for her a few days after my eleventh birthday.

I remember that birthday like it was yesterday because it truly was the best birthday I'd ever had. I was excited about the new clothes I was getting, sure, but what got me going the most was my brand new skateboard. Nope, no more banana-board for me, I had a professional looking board – but I only used it five times before I threw it in the bin. Why, you ask? Good question.

I was riding my new board in the street a couple of days after my birthday. I had my hat on, brand new Converse All-Star low-tops and, of course, my baggy jeans. Our house was on a cul-de-sac which made it easy to ride without having to worry about traffic. I was having so much fun, jumping the kerbs and practising the two or three tricks that I knew, when the oddest thing happened.

I must have been incredibly focused on what I was doing because I didn't notice the two girls – maybe a year or so older than me – walking around the cul-de-sac. I was startled by the sudden sound of laughter and it made me jump almost a foot off the ground. With my face as red as a tomato I managed to look over at them and smile. One of the girls was a redhead and the other a brunette. I remember that my stomach was in complete knots when they started talking to me.

'My friend thinks you're cute!' said the brunette.

I looked over at the redhead and smiled. Simultaneously she hit her friend playfully and waved at me in a sweet, bashful way.

I did wave back to her, but that wave brought so much confusion.

'What am I doing?' I remember thinking to myself, knowing that I was going to talk to this girl.

It was obvious that she thought I was a boy and I didn't deny it. Something was definitely wrong.

'What's your name?' I asked the redhead.

'Kara,' she said shyly.

'Pretty name.'

She turned away giggling when the brunette asked me, 'What's your name?'

'Uh... Ben.'

I couldn't believe that I was talking to two girls who thought I was a boy and on top of that, I'd told them that my name was Ben. The weird thing was, it felt good – almost natural – but at the same time it scared the hell out of me. Not just because I was pretending to be a boy, but because I thought Kara was the most beautiful girl I'd ever seen and when I looked at her I got a warm, fuzzy sensation inside.

The conversation ended quickly and the girls were walking away down the street. They occasionally looked back at me grinning.

I started to skate back to my house with a huge smile on my face. I was completely giddy – until I looked up and saw my mom standing on the front porch with the weirdest expression on her face. Suddenly the warm, fuzzy sensation was gone and my stomach felt like it was going to drop to the ground. I knew she'd heard everything.

I was an actress for the rest of that day, pretending like nothing had happened at all, and avoiding my mom. She didn't speak to me much for the rest of the day or night either.

I stayed in my room listening to music and thinking about the day. I felt uncomfortable because I didn't know what was happening to me and why it felt so good when I was talking to those girls. Especially Kara.

Around 10 o'clock that night I decided to venture into the kitchen to grab a drink. I walked down the stairs quietly, trying to avoid any confrontation with my mom. There was no confrontation, but I never did get that drink.

From just outside the kitchen, I could hear that my mom was talking in a soft whisper to someone over the phone, but I could still hear what she was saying and it was both unexpected and shocking.

'What do I do? I think she might be queer.'

I was stunned and couldn't move for what felt like hours. I fought back as hard as I could but the tears began to fall. They were flowing so easily and so much that I thought I might drown.

Before that night, I'd never cried so much, never hurt so deeply or experienced such inner turmoil. I felt so ashamed. I felt like I must be gross and weird. I wanted to crawl away and hide in a place where no one could find me. I felt like my mom hated me.

I am not queer and I will prove it to you I said to myself.

All I wanted was my mom to love me; I didn't want to embarrass her. So, I decided that night that I would have to change a little to make her realise that I *wasn't* queer.

I marched up to my room, grabbed my brand new skateboard and threw it in the bin. From that moment on, I never picked up another board.

That day stirred up many different emotions within me. I felt fear, sadness, disgust and shame, not to mention the anger that began to brew. The years that followed were incredibly hard, almost agonizing...

Jeez, look at the time! One more bite of this omelette and I'm out of here. I really can't be late – not today.

I wipe my mouth, stand up and toss my bag across my shoulders.

'See ya later, Mom.'

She is still engrossed in her newspaper, but manages to look at me with a little smile.

'Have a good first day at school.'

I walk over and give her a hug.

'I will. I should be home by four.'

'Okay, hon.'

As I walk to the front door I push back a laugh. Mom's getting better at giving hugs, but they are still a little loose. Everyone at some point has felt the unforgettable patting on the back hug. You know the one, right? It's where the other person is counting the seconds from the very beginning, waiting for the hug to be over. My mom isn't quite that bad but pretty darn close. When I was a kid she would give me the most comforting squeeze, now she seems to be avoiding the whole thing. Perhaps she is afraid she might catch it – the Gay Flu that is. I hear it's going around.

But my mom does seem to be getting better. One day I hope to feel her true embrace again. But until then, I have to joke about it with myself because now it just makes me laugh. I try to laugh often because if I don't, I will cry and I don't feel like I should have to cry anymore.

CHAPTER 3

The year before the skateboarding experience I was in the fifth grade. Truthfully, I think deep inside I knew even then that something was wrong with me. I say *wrong* with me because that is how I felt for the longest time. I know better now.

Primary school should have been a blast, as it usually is for so many other kids. You build friendships that sometimes last a lifetime and begin to find your own identity. I had no idea who I was or what I was doing, other than I had to go to school and do school work.

I was a loner who sat on the sidelines at break times. Not because I wanted to, but because everyone seemed to avoid me like the plague. I loved to climb the jungle gym and occasionally I would do just that, but always by myself. I mastered the ability to walk on the bars without holding on. At that age I swore to myself that I would join the circus because then I would be around other *freaks* like me. I know that that is an uncharitable thing to say, but that is what I thought back then.

Every day I would walk to school with my headphones on. We weren't allowed to have CD players or anything in school but I managed to hide it. I became an expert. I would tuck it underneath everything in my bag and put it in the little zipper compartment on the inside. I couldn't have lasted a day without my music; it was my therapy and the only thing that helped me deal with the world around me that seemed to reject me.

Once I got to school I would sit at my desk in complete silence. I would look around at the other kids who were having so much fun, talking and joking with one another. But I sat alone; no one said anything to me. Well, except for the occasional jokes. Not good laugh-your-ass-off jokes either; they were all aimed *at* me, making fun of the 'yucky' girl.

I hated that I was viewed as the 'yucky' girl but the sad thing is, I got used to it. I thought that one day they would all stop calling me that, so for a while I simply held onto the hope.

I put my energy into my homework and music. I started to draw a lot too, because it somehow made me feel better. I separated myself from so much and acted like I didn't have a care in the world when the truth is, I was hurting so badly inside.

When I was at school I talked to my teacher a lot. Well I tried to anyway. Her name was Ms Hammond. I always thought that she was so beautiful. She always smelled good too. Her long wavy brown hair was so shiny and her smile was like white pearls. Occasionally, when the class was going out for break, I would lag behind waiting for her. As we were walking outside, I'd hold the door open for her.

'You're pretty.' I would tell her.

She would smile and say thank you.

A few of my classmates heard me say that to Ms Hammond one day and they made fun of me for it. I was not only a 'yucky' girl, but a 'suck up' as well. I really wasn't sucking up to her; I just thought she was amazing. I hoped that one day I would look like her. I hated being ugly. Well, I hated to *feel* ugly. Some days were better than others, but most of the time the days were just horrible.

I remember one day in particular. Almost all the other girls had boyfriends; not anything serious, but still boyfriends. I really had no desire to have a boyfriend. I didn't get why it was such a big deal. In my mind, boys would be great friends, hanging out, maybe climbing a tree or two, but a *boyfriend* was something I didn't want.

That day though, I decided to try to get one, if only to see what all the fuss was about.

There was this boy in my class named Kenny. He wasn't really cute at all, but I didn't really care about that. He did have a lot of friends though, probably because he was the class clown. He was a goofy looking kid with glasses and had little sense of style. Half the time I just couldn't imagine what he was thinking, wearing the clothes he did. Well, that didn't matter to me.

I sat at my desk all morning, through our mathematics, social studies and art lessons, in a daze. My mind drifted away the entire time, with my eyes fixed on the blank notebook paper in front of me. I didn't take notes or do class work that day. I was trying to figure out how to ask Kenny to be my boyfriend. The thought grossed me out, but I thought that if I had a boyfriend maybe everyone else would start to like me.

By lunch I decided to ask him. I took my pencil and wrote him a letter on a piece of notebook paper.

Kenny

Will you go out with me? Check yes or no.

from Constance

At the end of the note I drew two boxes, one for yes and the other for no. I knew other kids made notes like that, so I thought it would be the best way to ask. Nice and simple.

I walked to the cafeteria slowly. I was totally nervous. I felt sick to my stomach and swore I was going to puke. Gross I know, but that is how I felt.

The lunch room was noisy as always, kids yelling, laughing and running around while some teacher tried to stop them or calm them down. Every day a different teacher was trying to accomplish that. They rarely succeeded.

I would normally take my lunch to a table and sit by myself. My lunch was always the same; a ham sandwich with mayonnaise. Thanks for having an imagination, Mom. I was sick and tired of ham sandwiches but I was always starving by lunchtime, so I always ate it anyway.

That day was different. I decided to walk over to Kenny's lunch table with the note in hand. My hair was actually looking okay that day too, because I hadn't been wearing a hat. I was hoping that fact would help persuade him to say yes.

His table was almost all boys and they were loud! I walked up behind him and tapped him on the back. I forced out a smile as he turned around and looked at me.

'Hey Kenny.'

'What do you want?' he said. He sounded kind of nasty.

'Um, nothing really. Just wanted to give you this.'

I held my hand out and gave him the note. He looked at the folded piece of paper for a moment without opening it and then looked over at his friends. They were laughing, sounding like a bunch of hyenas. I should have walked away but for some reason I just waited there, even as he opened the note and read it.

Kenny read it to himself first, and then aloud to his friends. He didn't read it in a normal tone either, it seemed like he was screaming, and surely loud enough so that half of the cafeteria could hear him.

It was so embarrassing, I felt my face getting hot and I started to sweat. I decided to just back off and walk away, far from the lunch room.

I stopped in my tracks when I heard Kenny yell after me.

'Constance!'

I stood there for a moment, not moving a muscle. I didn't know what to do, whether to run like a big baby or turn around and face him. So I turned around to find Kenny standing up by the lunch table with a stupid grin on his face.

'Nice note,' he said. 'But I thought you only liked girls, seeing as how you are a boy and all.'

Practically the entire room started laughing. I am probably exaggerating a little bit, but that's how it felt. It seemed like everyone's eyes and all the laughter was directed towards me.

I did not say anything back; I couldn't. I just turned slowly around and walked out of the cafeteria, trying my hardest not to cry. Actually, I didn't cry; I just walked away. And I didn't just walk away from the cafeteria; I walked down the hall and out of the school doors. I didn't want to go back to class, not then or ever.

When I went home that afternoon I didn't say much of anything to my mom. I stayed upstairs in my room, only coming down for dinner. I can't remember what we ate because I didn't eat more than two bites. I still felt sick to my stomach and just wanted to be alone. My mom tried to talk to me, but I only nodded or mumbled. She knew something was wrong, but didn't question me or anything. She just glanced over at me every now and then. It was like she was practically examining everything about me.

After dinner I went straight up to my room and turned on my CD player. I took a minute to search for a song that fit how I was feeling right at that moment.

I ended up listening to Tupac's Only God Can Judge Me. I turned up the volume louder than I probably should have, moving my head to the rhythm. I leaned back, falling onto the bed and sunk into my fluffy, cozy, duvet.

I remember lying there in the dark, listening to the music that was incredibly loud, yet somehow felt so faint and distant. My mind drifted completely. I was thinking about who I was, about how much I didn't understand my life. And didn't understand practically everything else around me, come to that.

I cried myself to sleep that night, praying that when I woke up in the morning, everything would be okay. I would be a well-liked, beautiful, normal kid with tons of friends... But obviously, that didn't happen.

CHAPTER 4

The route I walk to school is the same today as it has been for the last six years. The high school and junior school are practically parallel to one another. I never understood why because it makes it much easier for the older kids to bully the youngsters. Of course, I never have done the bullying, but I have seen it happen quite often. I wish there was something that I could do to stop it, but there isn't, which angers me.

Most of the time while I'm walking to school I have music blaring through my headphones. It is a way for me more or less to block out the world around me and go to my own imaginary place. Some days my imagination goes wild, but it can be entertaining.

Often I become completely entranced by the music and picture my life differently. I imagine myself full of creativity, moving up in the world fast and being successful. I imagine myself genuinely happy. These thoughts make me smile, but when I return to reality I sometimes become depressed and nervous about what my future may hold.

When I am not daydreaming about my own life, I find it interesting to people-watch and spot people who are actually walking to the beat of the music. I wonder how their lives are and what they are thinking about at that moment. Are they happy, sad, angry or overwhelmed? I wonder where they are going as well, I make up little stories about them in my mind.

Today I started off the same way, with my headphones on, but for some reason I decided to take them off. I am in such a great mood and it feels good to hear the world around me. I hear people talking and laughing and the occasional car horn. I am not sure why, but I feel refreshed.

Quite often I feel invisible, like I don't even exist. I even felt that way yesterday; but today I realise that people are walking by with smiles on their faces, looking at *me*.

I can't lie, sometimes the way people look at me *does* bother me and it can hurt. Surprisingly though, today any negative attention I receive doesn't bother me so much. My mind is clear and I figure that anyone judging me just doesn't get the fact that everyone on this planet is different in some way. If we were all alike, life would be boring and there would be no thrill. Well, that's how I see it anyway.

I think I realised that I was practically invisible when I was in sixth grade. I knew that my mom loved me but after the night when I'd overheard her on the phone, I felt she started to act funny. She would talk to me but she seemed distant.

When I mention the past to her now, she insists that she wasn't distant from me, but I know better. It really affected me in a negative way, causing me to feel like the whole world was against me; and that I was totally alone. And it must have been my fault; after all, if my own mother treated me weird there had to have been something wrong with me.

Out of all of those years at school, sixth grade was probably the worst. Well, at least half of that year anyway. My experience with Kenny the year before made sure that I was the laughing stock of the entire school. And when I say entire school, I mean *entire* school – even the fourth graders walked by laughing at me. I know it probably wasn't *completely* horrible, looking back, but it *was* bad. I think I was drained emotionally, so that every little hill seemed like a gigantic mountain.

On my first day of sixth grade I remember going into class and sitting down at a desk in the front row. I sat down next to a couple of girls, ones I'd actually never seen before.

Thinking that they were possibly new to the school and had no idea who I was, I decided to try to talk to them. I had good intentions and hoped that maybe, just maybe, I could make a friend or two – but I was wrong. Just as I sat down, they looked over at me, whispered something to each other and moved to different desks.

Every day at school that year I was avoided and ignored by most of my classmates. Occasionally someone would ask me for help with a maths problem or homework assignment, but nothing ever personal. I sat at my desk with my eyes fixed on my notepaper, my book or my teacher, Ms Tuttle.

Ms Tuttle was an interesting teacher, very enthusiastic and always happy. I wondered how it felt to be happy every day and always smiling. She reminded me of myself in a small way. Not her personality, but how she dressed and walked. She never wore dresses, just suits, and her hair was short. She was nice and tried to talk to me but I never felt confident enough, unless it was to answer a question in class.

However, things changed for me four weeks before that school year ended. That day I was sitting as I normally did, with my eyes fixed on my notebook.

'Class listen up,' Ms Tuttle said.

I was listening, but not looking up at her.

'I know it is late in the year, but I want you to welcome Kara. She will be joining our class for the remainder of the year.'

When I heard that name my heart practically dropped into my stomach. I knew a girl named Kara - well at least I had for a few minutes earlier that year.

I looked up and there she was, standing in front of the class, smiling. It *was* the Kara I'd met that day when I was skateboarding. She looked over at me and smiled; I grinned back nervously, but immediately looked back down at my paper and began doodling. Inside I felt sick, giddy and nervous simultaneously. I didn't know what to do with myself. She thought that I was a boy and she was going to find out that I wasn't, and probably hate me like everyone else did. I didn't want that.

Ms Tuttle told Kara that she could sit anywhere that she wanted to. I thought for sure that she would sit far away from me, but she walked over to the desk next to mine and sat down. I glanced up at her and realised that she was looking at me and smiling.

'Can I sit here?'

'Sure,' I said shyly, looking back down at my paper.

Even so, Kara and I didn't say much to each other for about two weeks. The occasional 'Hi' in the morning was about it. She would try to make conversation with me but I avoided it. I was so embarrassed.

One day I was sitting in the lunch room, by myself of course, when she came over to my table and sat down. She didn't say anything for a minute, just started to lay her lunch out on the table and took a bite of her sandwich. After a while, she looked up at me.

'It's cool if I sit here?' she asked.

'Sure.'

I wanted to talk to her, but didn't have a clue what to say. I was used to being talked *at*, not talking *with* anyone. At that time I wasn't sure whether she was being nice to me because she wanted to, or whether she was going to make fun of me later, like everyone else did.

The background noise of the lunch room seemed to cave in on us for a moment as we sat there in total silence. Even though we weren't saying one word to each other, it still felt good to sit with someone.

'I am not sure if I like this school yet,' she said, sort of breaking the ice.

'Yeah, I don't really like it either,' I said with a smile.

'Did we meet before? Before I came to this school?'

I sat there not knowing what to say. I just looked at her. I remember almost panicking because I didn't know how to respond, so I decided to just lie.

'Don't think so.'

'Really? Because you look familiar.'

I felt like an idiot because all I could come back with was 'Uh.'

'Well it's nice to meet you...' She paused for a moment. 'What's your name again?'

'Constance.'

'Oh yeah,' she said with a smile.

After that short conversation, we sat and ate our lunch, talking about little things. She told me that she had just moved across town and had to switch schools, and that she hated to leave all of her friends.

It was difficult for her to enroll in a school where she didn't know anyone at all. We talked about our favourite music, movies and video games, finding that we had a lot in common.

That day at lunch was the best day I'd had in years and one I will always remember. I felt so happy and warm inside, knowing that someone liked me for who I was. Especially Kara, because she knew I'd lied to her earlier that year. The funny thing is, even to this day she has never brought it up.

For the rest of my sixth grade year, Kara and I hung out together everyday. We ate lunch together, talked about everything and even went to the mall a couple of times on the weekend. I finally knew how it felt to have a friend, a best friend, someone I could tell everything. Well, almost everything.

I was excited because we were going to the same middle school the following year. To go into a new school meant a new beginning for me and going with a newly found friend made it seem even better.

I promised myself that I would change a bit before going into seventh grade. I was going to ask my mom to buy me some new clothes. I wanted outfits that were nice looking, but nothing too girlie. I wanted to be liked, to make friends and be normal. For some reason, back then I thought that changing the way I dressed would help matters. Just thinking about that transition to seventh grade makes me a tad uneasy.

Today I feel the same nervousness that I felt on my first day of middle school. Even though I am going back to school and will be surrounded by students I am familiar with, I have changed a lot since last year. I have gained a sense of pride and strength, which I hope will stay with me. I don't want to lose what I have worked so hard for, once I walk through those doors. I am almost positive that I won't break, but the thought of that possibility is lingering with me.

I will be all right.

CHAPTER 5

The summer following my sixth grade year is one of the best memories I have, although it passed all too quickly. The almost 12 weeks of the summer break seemed like a mere two. Previously, I'd have been counting the days until school started again. I'd usually be tired of hanging around by myself all the time. And I'd be thinking, at least if I were in school I'd have homework to occupy me. Being bored and *alone* was the worst.

That summer following sixth grade, Kara and I became the best of friends. We were practically inseparable. I don't think we spent one day apart and almost every night either I stayed at her house or she stayed at mine.

We talked about pretty much everything. We even played war games together, which was odd because most other girls disliked those sorts of things.

It turned out that Kara was like me, a tomboy, and she didn't speak once about having a crush on a boy. It was refreshing to be around someone that I could be *real* with; I didn't have to worry about being embarrassed for wanting to throw a football around or climb a tree. Because we did those things together. The only real difference between Kara and me was the fact that she dressed more like a girl. And I never once saw her wear a baseball cap.

My mom got used to having Kara around and liked her. Occasionally if Kara and I were in my room, my mom would pop her head around the door for a moment unannounced. I think now that she was wondering if we were really *just* friends and was simply trying to catch us out.

I don't know what she thought we would have been doing at that age. Why my mom would have thought we'd be doing anything is beyond me. But I guess moms know everything, right? I never once vocalized it to her, but maybe she could read my body language and my facial expressions. I was just pure happiness whenever Kara was around.

Inside though, I knew that what I felt for Kara was maybe more than I should have been feeling. And that horrified me. It made me feel that I was bonkers or something – but I kept that to myself. I wanted to enjoy our friendship, not act like a crazy person.

I remember the day when I realised that I might have more feelings for Kara than I really wanted to admit. It was late in the summer vacation and we were in my room, sitting in front of the TV, playing a video game. It was the best fighting game ever because the player could morph into just about anything it wanted to, to hide from an opponent. Anyway, Kara was losing, which made her laugh as usual.

'I'm tellin' ya Con... I suck at this game.'

'Nah you don't; you're just having a bad luck day today.'

I wasn't looking at her; I was still staring at the TV screen.

'You almost beat me.'

'Yeah right.'

Kara slapped my leg jokingly. And she let her hand sit there for a minute. She was still laughing and looking right at me. I was trying to focus on the game, forcing a smile and avoiding looking back at her.

As her hand lay there I felt a strange sensation flow through my entire body. Suddenly I felt everything in my body jolt, not on the outside but inside. It was like an electric current was passing through me, but it wasn't painful at all; it just felt right.

I stopped moving my hands; I couldn't play the game anymore. I felt as stiff as a board and almost panicked but didn't want Kara to notice or anything. After all, I was sure it was just a friendly gesture. I mean, we hugged each other good-bye all the time, so that moment of her hand resting on my leg couldn't have meant anything on her part. It was just me – I was screwed up.

'Man! I can't believe it! I was so close!' I was trying to ignore the feeling I had inside.

Kara moved her hand, looked at the TV screen and then at me.

'Wanna play again?'

'We can if you want, maybe you'll actually beat me for once!'

We played the same video game over and over again for a couple of hours. All night though, I couldn't shake the feeling I'd had earlier. I was trying hard just to be myself. Kara asked me once if anything was wrong and I told her no, that I just had a slight headache.

That night she didn't stay over. I felt like I needed to be by myself. I wanted to lie on my bed and think; probably cry and yell at myself – which I did. I was scared and felt lost *again*. I loved having Kara as my friend but wasn't sure if I would be able to look at her the same way.

I didn't know what to do, so I spent the next day playing sick. I stayed in my room all day, only leaving to go to the bathroom and eat. Kara called at the house for me and I spoke to her only briefly, playing sick. I told her that I would probably feel better the next day and we could hang out then.

The next day and for the remainder of the summer holiday we were together, playing and joking around as usual. I had a small wall up, but it was nothing obvious. Well, at least I thought not.

Even if I didn't bring up that day, I surely thought about it. I even dreamt about it. The dreams disturbed me and I couldn't understand why I was having dreams about Kara. Nothing gross or anything, they were just happy – really happy.

A week or so before school was due to start, my mom and I went to the mall to buy me some new clothes. They were cute and surely going to help start the year off right. I was determined to be normal for once and to be liked. I also planned on having a boyfriend.

The idea of having a boyfriend wasn't a great thought, but I didn't care. I wanted more or less to make a point to my mom, to Kara and to myself – the point being that I was just like everyone else. After all, I was about to turn 13 and all the other girls seemed to have boyfriends. So, I made my mind up that by the fourth week of school I was going to have one of my own, no matter what. I wasn't concerned about looks, so finding one wouldn't be that hard I reckoned.

I kept my plan top secret, so when the time came I would *act* surprised and excited to everyone around me, even though I wouldn't be. I decided I had to have certain restrictions though, and wrote them down in my journal. I certainly wasn't going to kiss whoever it was – just the thought of it made me feel ill. But I decided a hug and holding hands on occasion would be okay.

The day before school started I was a nervous wreck. The entire day I played 'what-if' scenarios through my head. I was torturing my mind and emotional state so that I became full of negativity. I tried to remain calm and level-headed, but it wasn't happening. I think I had my first panic attack that day, my heart racing, sweat pouring from my body. I could have sworn that I was having a heart attack.

Kara came over to my house that day to show me her new school things. For some reason, as kids we found a strange pleasure in new notebooks and pencils. Kara was excited and could not wait for school to start. She was rambling on and on about how the following day might go, and I could tell by her voice that she was thrilled. However, she stopped talking when she realised the state I was in.

We talked for a while; well, she talked mostly. She tried to convince me that everything was going to be okay and that this new school year would be different from the others. I wanted to believe her, but it was hard. Going to a brand new school meant a new environment and new students, which only made me uneasy.

Later that night Kara and I talked on the phone and the conversation actually eased my mind. I couldn't go to school being so negative. I had to act as if everything was fine and there was nothing to worry about.

I tossed and turned that night, unable to sleep at all. I woke up early, two hours earlier than I had to, to get dressed. I wanted to do my hair perfectly, have my outfit look the best it could, as well as my make-up. First impressions mean a lot and I knew that, even at that age.

I remember wishing that I was able to talk to my mom about my worries, but I couldn't. I had this constant feeling that she was judging me, even if she actually wasn't. I was afraid to tell her how nervous I was about going to school, and why. She didn't really know about how I'd been treated the previous years. Just little things here and there; but not everything. If I had made her aware of some of the horrible things I'd been through, she would have been so upset. So today I decided to keep my fears to myself – for a while.

I met Kara at her house and we walked together. My palms were sweaty and I was hugely anxious. But knowing that I wasn't going alone helped a lot. Kara kept my mind occupied as she talked away about the new year, the classes we were going to be taking, the excitement of having a locker and how she could not wait to dissect frogs. I was excited about the lockers and having seven different classrooms instead of one, but not dissecting frogs or any other thing – yuck!

Today as I walk to school I have the all-too-familiar sweaty palms again, but that is about it. My nerves are steady for the most part. And after all, I should be excited; this is my last year of school! Then I will be going to college, possibly move away. The start of my life. My new life.

Kara promised me that she would meet me at the gymnasium doors. She has a car and I don't, so I have to walk. Some days she will pick me up, but most of the time she doesn't, but only because she has a habit of being late. I hope that today she is on time; preferably early.

We have our first, second and third classes of the day together, which is great. Sometimes it is hard being in the same class with Kara, because we tend to laugh and joke and pass notes the entire time. Last year I received at least five after-school detentions because of that. She only received one, which proves that she is better at masking her behaviour than me. And we hung out so much outside of school that you'd think that we wouldn't need to talk throughout a whole class period. But we did.

CHAPTER 6

The first couple weeks of seventh grade were a bit odd. It was hard for me to separate myself from the past and realise that my life at school could be different; it didn't always have to be a horrible experience. For those two weeks I mostly kept to myself, talking only to Kara.

Every morning I spent at least an hour getting ready. My clothes had to be perfect; perfectly matched and wrinkle-free. My shoes matched every single outfit as well, which I was secretly proud of. I enjoyed wearing make-up for the first time and looking more girlie. I would look in the mirror some days and be amazed because I actually *felt* cute.

Kara and I would hang out together at lunch everyday. I would watch her as she talked to various girls at the tables next to us. Somehow she always seemed to end up part of a long, drawn-out conversation. I didn't mind it; occasionally I would laugh and jump in myself but, of course, only saying a word or two. Even though there was a ton of things I wanted to say, I just couldn't – and that aggravated me, the fact that I was afraid of looking like an idiot.

A month into classes I felt a change come over me – and for the better, or so I thought. The change wasn't anything drastic, it was more internal. And it paved the way for me to be able to show the outside world more of my *true* self.

The change was sudden, like it happened overnight, and I don't know what sparked it. I started to talk a little more with the kids Kara talked to. I would find myself laughing at things that I normally wouldn't have laughed at. I knew that I wasn't going to be good friends with those kids and really I didn't want to be; I had no real desire to be friends with kids who made fun of me the year before. But talking to them during the school day was okay with me.

I didn't forget about the secret promise I had made to myself either, and I ended up getting a boyfriend by the end of the first month at school. I almost changed my mind about that, but I stuck with it even though I had my reservations. But in the hallways at school there were always plenty of girls with boys, holding hands, so I figured, why not?

In my third period maths class there was this kid named Sean. He was a little dorky-looking, wearing glasses and smart trousers to school every day. I didn't find him cute or anything but I did like his sense of style, so that helped persuade me. We were also in a band together. He played the clarinet and I played the drums. That amused me. Somehow I thought our roles should be switched, but I had no interest in playing the clarinet. And anyway, banging on a drum made me happy; it released some tension and took me to a far away place.

One day I just decided to ask Sean out. I was dressed extra nice that day and felt good. I tried to be casual about it, not wanting Kara to see me pass him the note. Why was that such a big deal? Well, I didn't want her to see me because I wanted her to think that *he* had asked *me* out. I had the note prewritten, with the two boxes marked 'yes' or 'no'. And while Kara's head was buried in her maths book, I passed it to him.

I sat at my desk looking at Sean every now and then, waiting for a reply. It seemed like he was reading the note over and over again and I didn't understand why because it was only one sentence. I remember thinking, is it such a hard decision? But right after I'd had that thought, he wrote something down on the paper and passed it back to me. Just as I took the note from him I looked over at Kara. She was fixing me with a quizzical look. I gave her an exaggerated smile and shrugged my shoulders.

I looked at the unopened note on my desk for a few minutes, unsure of how I would feel if it said either yes or no. I didn't really want a boyfriend, so if it *had* said no, would I have been upset? Well possibly, because I guess I would have thought I was repulsive to everyone, or something like that. But, as it happened, he said *yes* and included his phone number in the note.

After class that day I wore a fake smile that practically stretched from ear to ear and told Sean that I would call him. I knew Kara had witnessed the entire thing and I was well aware of the fact that she would immediately begin to badger me about what was going on with him.

She ran up to me with a huge smile on her face, mad with excitement and curiosity. She had never seen me talk to a boy, let alone see one pass me a note.

'What was that all about?' she asked.

I smirked at her and tried to walk around her, trying to act all cool.

'Oh, nothing really.'

'Yeah, right! He was passing you a note. I saw him.'

'It's not a big deal; it was just a short letter,' I told her. 'He told me he really liked me.'

Kara was walking incredibly fast, trying to keep up with me. Inside I was laughing because she was acting in an entirely different way than I was used to.

'Oh my God! What else? Huh?'

'Okay, okay! Jeez! He asked me out.'

I stopped to gauge her reaction.

'Wow! And you said yes?'

'Sure why not?'

'Um, I don't know, you just never seemed to care about stuff like that.'

There was a curious tone to her voice.

'Yeah, well it's time for that now, I guess. He's, uh, kinda cute, y'know?'

'Well, great!'

I knew that she wasn't as excited as she pretended to be, and I wasn't sure why. Even so, we talked about Sean during the entire break. Kara continued to ask me a ton of questions about him and made me promise to call her right after he and I had talked that night. I told her I would. To be honest, I didn't want to talk about Sean any more and was relieved when I got to my next class.

I was interested in biology and I was making an 'A', but that day I could not focus. My mind was wandering. I thought about Kara and wondered if she was going to have a boyfriend of her own soon. For some reason, I didn't like the thought of her having one. It bothered me. I was sure that she was okay with me going steady with Sean, so why should I care if she met someone? It didn't make any sense. I also thought about Sean and how the 'going steady' thing would work, because I wasn't sure. Really though, we were just in seventh grade so it couldn't be that serious, right?

Anyway, Sean seemed like a cool kid and I was sure I could be friends with him at least for a while. In my mind I was hoping that we would do fun things together – play basketball and stuff like that. I didn't in any way, shape or form want to do *anything* mushy. Yuck.

That night I called him. It took me about an hour to dial the number all the way through and wait for him to answer. I had no idea what I was going to say and didn't want to sit with the receiver up to my ear saying nothing at all. But we actually talked for about 45 minutes about nothing in particular. We talked about our band and the concert that was coming up, and gym class and other kids from school. It really wasn't a bad conversation, but I did find it just a little uncomfortable when he told me how much he liked me. When he told me that I fell silent for a moment, because I didn't know what to say back. I wasn't going to lie and tell him I liked him a lot too, was I? Well yes, I did just that. I felt bad about it, but just couldn't help myself.

The following weeks and months of school were great. I was still going steady with Sean of course, but didn't mind it because we were more like friends. Well, friends who occasionally held hands. He did kiss me on the cheek once after school, and actually that turned out to be okay. It wasn't as gross as I thought it would be. Kara and I still hung out everyday as well. At lunch we sat together with Sean and a few other girls that Kara was friendly with.

By the end of the school year I had two things that I never in a million years thought I would ever have. I had friends, *and* a boyfriend. The friends weren't really close friends though; just kids I talked to in school. Kara was still my best friend and Sean was becoming a close friend as well, and actually that was enough for me.

Outwardly, things were great and it felt good to be fitting in more and to be liked. Even so, there was inner turmoil that played on my mind. It was like something was telling me that I'd somehow lost sight of what was really important. My school work began to suffer too. I was slacking big-time and I didn't care. I had finally got what I thought I really wanted.

I had become the class clown, which had helped me gain some more friends, but had landed me in detention at least every other day. I loved making people laugh and loved the fact that they were laughing at what I said or did, rather than laughing at me.

Still, that nagging in the back of my mind would bring on an occasional depression. I realised that I didn't want to be Sean's girlfriend any more, but I still wanted to be his friend. I wasn't spending as much time with Kara because I was spending time with Sean, and I missed Kara terribly. She and I did talk on the phone all the time, but it just wasn't the same.

In a way I became lost, waiting to be found – or waiting to find myself, I should say.

CHAPTER 7

First day of ninth grade. As I walk closer to the gymnasium doors I spot Kara leaning against them. She is dressed nicely as always, wearing a free-flowing skirt and tank top which match each other precisely. Her hair is pulled back and looks really glamorous and her red coloured lipstick is glistening in the morning sun. In my opinion, Kara is just a truly wonderful person. She has a magical personality that can make even the worst of days seem fabulous. I only have to hear her soothing voice for a minute or two and all is fine with the world.

Looking at Kara, I feel kind of strange, and for some reason temporarily nauseous.

It's a feeling that sometimes comes over me when I look at her and I can't explain why. And although it's nausea, I don't feel bad or anything.

I wave at Kara and walk quickly over to her. I try to look cool on the outside, but I know that Kara can always see right through me.

'Hey girlie! Looking nice,' Kara says to me.

I look at her and smile, and suddenly I'm at ease, just like that. I look down at my clothes briefly, then eye up her rock-star apparel.

'Thanks. You look good yourself. New outfit?'

'Of course! Isn't that what you would expect of me, first day back?' she says, giggling.

'Right,' I say as we begin walking towards school doors. 'I'm glad you showed up. I was nervous you would be late. Again.'

Kara smacks me on the shoulder jokingly while strolling along next to me. I'm always teasing her about her time-keeping. She's not late *all* the time. But it's a joke we like to share.

'Jeez Con! I'm not *that* bad am I?'

'Umm yeah, sometimes you are,' I say with a smile. 'But I am so glad you made it today. Thanks.'

As she smiles, her eyes look me over again. I know what she is thinking. *Why are you so worked up about this? You are awesome and you will be okay.* Her gaze tells me just that. And yes, I will be okay – with Kara by my side. I would be okay by myself as well, I'm sure, but having her around definitely helps.

Ninth grade was my last year at middle school. And it was the year that I realised that Kara could turn my rainy days into days full of sunshine.

Sean and I had been dating for almost two years. Our relationship wasn't anything serious at all really, because I avoided taking things to a deeper level. I did realise that it bothered him, but I didn't care.

Every day I did the same thing. I walked to school with Kara and we met Sean by our lockers. He would always insist on holding my hand and I would for a minute or two, but then found reasons not to. I liked him as a person, just not as anything more. So the time came when I needed to break things off with him, and it happened sooner than I thought it would.

One day, about a month into the school year, we were all sitting at the lunch table talking, just laughing and joking around. I wasn't talking to Sean much, giving my attention to Kara and Rose, the girl Kara was talking with.

Rose was a pretty girl and new to the school. From the first day, she and Kara were pretty close, which I didn't like at all. Normally it wouldn't have been a big deal, but I thought it was odd that Kara didn't ever have a boyfriend and still wasn't interested in finding one. Rose didn't have a boyfriend either, and it appeared that they liked each other. I knew that it was rude to ignore Sean, but I wanted to hear everything that Kara and Rose were talking about. Was it possible that Kara liked girls? No way!

As I was listening into their conversation Sean began to pat me on the shoulder. It wasn't a pleasant way to get my attention either; he was determined to pat me until I looked in his direction. After a few minutes I finally gave in, but my irritation was apparent.

'What the hell do you want? Can't you see I'm talking?' I yelled at him.

He looked shocked, as if he couldn't believe I'd snapped at him.

'Oh, uh, I didn't think you were talking to them. Just wanted to ask you something that's all.'

I felt the anger boiling inside me and I couldn't help it. I didn't want to talk to him.

'What then?'

'Well, I was just wondering if you have thought about us at all? If you might want to...' he paused for a moment, appearing nervous, which only aggravated me more.

'Want to what?' I said.

'You know, take our relationship to another level?'

They were awkward words for a kid to say, and he sat there patiently, waiting for an answer. I was stunned, and it showed.

'What do you mean by that?'

'I don't know, see each other more or...'

'No, actually.' I said cutting him off.

At that time I was so angry that I didn't think about what I was saying to him. I didn't even realise that I was talking a bit louder than I should have been. Kara and Rose were looking over at us.

'I don't think we should see each other any more,' I blurted out.

'What?' he asked, completely shocked.

'Yeah, I've been thinking about it for a while. It's probably best.'

I knew that Sean was going to continue to ask me a ton of questions, but I just wanted to leave, so I did. I just stood up and looked right at him.

'I gotta go. I'll talk to you later,' I said.

Kara looked up at me.

'What are you doing?' she whispered to me.

'Nothin'! I just gotta go. Don't worry about me; just stay here with your little friends.'

After that I stormed out of the lunch room, leaving both Kara and Sean utterly confused, but I didn't care. I walked as quickly as I could to my locker, not worried about how loud I was being, even though a few classes were in session. I flung open my locker door with a bang, pulled a few of my books out and threw them onto the top of the locker. I stood there looking at nothing, tears streaming down my face. I wanted to push them far away; I didn't want to be crying. As I stood there my anger took hold of me. I punched the locker two times, hard, so that the sound echoed throughout the empty hallway. My hand was bleeding, tears were falling, and I was angry and I had no idea why.

I gathered up my books, lying on top of the lockers, while I wiped my hand on my trousers. It was a disgusting thing to do, but I had nothing else to wipe the blood off with. I turned to close the door of my locker when I heard my name being called. It was Kara running down the hall towards me.

'Con, what's going on? Are you ok?'

I didn't respond for a moment, just looked at her as she approached me.

'What did you do?' she said as she picked up my arm, examining my hand.

'Nothing, I'm fine.'

'You are not! You better go to the nurse!'

'I'm going home,' I said, as I took my hand back and walked past her.

'Why? Constance come here!'

'I'll call you later,' I mumbled.

I walked slowly down the hallway towards the school doors. I heard Kara walking behind me, quietly. I felt bad for treating her that way, but I needed to get away from everything. I hated school. Right then, I didn't care for much of anything any more.

Just as I was about to turn the corner at the end of the locker hall, a voice called out.

'Hold it, you two!'

As I turned to face the voice, Kara did the same. It was a maths teacher whose class was in session near to my locker. He was an older man, probably close to 60 years old. The hair that he had left on his head was grey, but mostly he was bald. He didn't look one little bit friendly.

'What's going on out here?'

Kara looked over at me.

'Nothing sir,' Kara said. 'We were just grabbing some things from our lockers.'

'Sounded like *something*,' he said, noticing my bloody hand. 'What's your name?'

'Why?' I asked him.

'You want a visit to the Head? What is your name?'

'Send me where ya wanna. I don't care,' I replied with attitude.

'Constance just *tell* him.' Kara said.

'Oh, Constance is it? I believe I have heard your name somewhere. Well, get yourself to the front office.'

'Nah. I don't think I will.'

'Really? Then I will just have to take a break from my class and walk you there myself.'

I didn't respond to him, but did walk with him to the office. Kara followed beside us on her way back to the lunch room. She looked at me the entire way. She seemed concerned. I knew that I would be getting a phone call from her later on that night.

The rest of that day was spent in the Head's office. My teachers sent up my class work and my mother was called – just great. I was given an out-of-school suspension for three days for my actions in the hallway and for disrespecting the maths teacher.

I knew I would not hear the end of it that night from my mother, and I didn't. I chose to lock myself away in my room after listening to an hour-long lecture – well, it started out as a lecture but ended up a roaring fight. I screamed at her, telling her to leave me alone, then finally ran to my room, slamming the door behind me. I then blared out my music for the rest of the night, ignoring requests from my mother to turn it down.

Kara called me that night, but I didn't answer. I wasn't ready to talk about my psychotic episode in school (that is what it felt like) and I was embarrassed. I was sure she would call me the following day and we would talk about everything; even *I* didn't know what had caused my anger to surface in the way that it did. That kind of scared me too.

I knew that talking to Kara about my issues with Sean would be difficult, but I would easily be able to tell her about my day in the front office. I had been placed on a Behaviour and Homework Chart. As it turned out, a few of my teachers had reported my 'disruptive' classroom behaviour to the Head along with my lower than average grades. So from then on, until both issues improved, my mom had to sign the chart and keep tabs on me.

The following night I talked to Kara for at least two hours and apologised to her almost a dozen times. She finally told me to stop apologising and that it wasn't a big deal. It was an easy-going conversation and she didn't try to pry or force me to talk about anything I didn't want to. She simply made it known that she would be there for me if I ever needed to talk. That meant a lot to me.

It was during that conversation that I realised that Kara had a special effect on me. She could make me feel okay when I was sad or angry or depressed. I couldn't work out how or why, but that didn't matter.

Better than that, I knew for certain that no matter what, she would always be there for me. I was truly thankful for that – and I still am. They say that in life, things have to get more difficult before they get better, right? I must say in my case that was very true indeed.

The summer break between my ninth and tenth grade years was nothing extraordinary.

CHAPTER 8

My days were spent either hanging around at home in my room, or with Kara. The only difference was that Rose spent quite a bit of time with Kara and me. We all went to the mall together, went to the local adventure park to play laser tag together, or to the movies.

Rose was a nice girl and I didn't mind being friends with her at all. At times she was actually very funny. The only thing I was unsure of was how I felt about her and Kara's relationship. At times I caught them giggling with each other like they were sharing a secret — like the way a *couple* would giggle together. And then I realized that they were more than just friends when I caught the two of them holding hands one day.

Rose, Kara and I were sitting outside on my porch towards the end of the summer. We were chatting away about the school year to come, drinking Coca-Cola and joking around. We were all running low on drinks, so I decided to go inside and get the pitcher of juice along with some crisps.

I was inside the house for about five minutes, because my mother insisted on talking my ear off. At that time I didn't talk to my mother often. I actually went out of my way to avoid her. When we did talk it always seemed to end with us bickering. Anyway, that day we didn't fight, but I just wanted to get away from her and get back outside with my friends just the same.

Outside, Kara and Rose were practically snuggled up to one another, their hands intertwined, looking into each other's eyes. At first they didn't realise I was there, so I stood briefly with my jaw dropping to the floor. After a moment, I cleared my throat to draw attention to my presence. They quickly pushed away from each other, trying to act like they weren't doing anything at all.

I gave the two of them a crooked smile, and then sat down on the bench without saying a word. We were all silent for a while until Kara threw in an icebreaker by talking about the upcoming year and going to high school. It worked I guess, and I worked hard at acting normal – but my insides were crawling.

I felt angry, sad and jealous all at the same time. I knew deep down that I too wanted to snuggle with Kara; I wanted to hold her hand and have her look at me in *that* way. Yet in another way, I was angry with myself for actually feeling that way towards her. I didn't *want* to like girls. I wanted to be normal – but, I also realised, right there and then, that I didn't want to fool myself any longer.

At that very moment, questions played through my mind. Was I queer? Was I gay or weird? Was it okay that I might be gay? No! There was no way that I was! I was just feeling jealous over my best friend because she'd found a new best friend, right? I just couldn't be... I wouldn't allow myself to be gay.

I was so confused about the feelings churning inside me. What I *did* decide was to be more like my *old* self again. That mostly entailed getting back to wearing clothes that I'd always felt most comfortable in – meaning baggier. And comfort is what I wanted right then. Screw what other people thought about my style. What did it matter to them anyway?

In August, when I went to my new high school, I was back to my old self – almost. Kara and I walked to school together on the first day, and we also had the same class schedule, which was convenient. The first day, week and even month were great. My grades were pretty decent and I got along with most of the students. I did get the occasional remark about how I was dressed, but I tried hard to ignore them.

Kara and Rose were not dating each other any more, and Rose was still attending classes at the middle school, so we didn't hang out with her often. The two of them still talked and were friends, but not *together*. It was obvious that Kara was hurting over the break-up, even if she tried to deny it. She wouldn't talk to me about many details either, for some reason. All she told me was that Rose *freaked* out. I guessed 'freaked out' meant that she couldn't handle the truth about herself – which I completely understood – but I didn't dare express that to Kara.

During the second month of school certain events took place that caused me to spiral downhill emotionally and mentally. At that point my grades were average and once again I wasn't worried about how I was doing in school. I was still required to have my mother fill out a homework chart every night, but due to my good behaviour, I didn't need the behaviour chart any more.

One night after I got home from school my mother and I got into an argument. To this day I am not sure what caused it, but it was probably the worst one we had ever had. Our dinner that night was a weird combination, macaroni and beef, corn and a side salad. I was not fond of the food and remained silent as I ate. My mother kept trying to make eye contact with me, obviously wanting to start a conversation – one I knew I didn't want any part of.

'So honey, how was school?' she finally asked me.

I continued to poke at my food and didn't look up at her.

'It was okay,' I said, looking at my plate.

'Meeting any new friends?'

'Some,' I replied.

There was a moment of awkward silence between the two of us before my mother decided to try again.

'Meet any nice boys? I bet there are tons of cute ones,' she said with a grin.

I suddenly became tense throughout my entire body. I really disliked it when she asked me questions like that, because I knew what she was thinking deep down. *Is my daughter gay?* I often tried to talk about boys in front of her, because I knew it would make her doubt what I was sure she saw within me. Immediately I became defensive.

'Mom, why do you always have to ask me about boys? Boys, boys, boys. Is that all you think about? Why don't you get off my case? It's my life!' I yelled.

She looked startled, like she couldn't believe I'd reacted like that.

'I wasn't trying to get on your case, Constance. I'm just curious about your life, that's all.'

'Well I don't care! Don't ask me again! I can't stand that!'

I stopped eating my food; I felt really angry and couldn't help it. I stood up, picked up my plate and before I could stop myself, threw it against the wall. The food flew all over the kitchen; the plate shattered and fell to the floor. I stormed out of the kitchen and went up to my room, not even cleaning up the mess I'd made. While stomping up the stairs, I heard my mom yelling at me to clean up my mess.

'You do it!' I yelled down to her and stormed into my room, slamming the door behind me.

That was the first time I'd reacted like that, so badly that I couldn't control my temper. But it wasn't the last.

The next morning my mother barely talked to me, which was good because I was still upset about the night before. I left the house without saying goodbye to her, and walked to school alone, feeling churned up inside.

All day I was in a horrible mood. I talked to Kara and we joked around a bit, but I was still unnerved. I didn't talk to her about the big blow out I'd had with my mother, so I avoided talking about the night before. I knew I could talk to Kara about anything and I probably would have told her the details, but I didn't want her to think I was psychotic for throwing a plate. She probably wouldn't have thought that – yet still I didn't dare mention it.

I stopped caring about school altogether. In each of my classes, I fell asleep almost completely and didn't do any work. I was just tired, had a lack of energy, didn't care and couldn't focus. My thoughts led me into daydreams about myself, about who I was and where I was going. In my mind, my future looked grim and unpromising.

I received three after-school detentions in one day for sleeping and not participating in class. And I was sent to the office a couple times for mouthing off to a teacher. I also avoided contact with other students; I couldn't be bothered and I knew I wasn't in the frame of mind to talk to anyone. I was angry at myself and angry with life in general.

My bag was torn and I hadn't been able to get a new one yet, so I had to carry all my books in my arms. As I was leaving school their weight began to get to me and I lost my grip, so that they fell to the ground. This cocky senior boy walked past me laughing, practically pointing. At what, I am still not sure, because people drop books all the time. Anyway, his sneering laugh irritated me and as I was picking my books up, I snapped.

'What the hell are you laughing at?' I asked, standing up. My insides began to tremble, not out of fear but anger.

'You talking to me?' he asked, and then he turned to his buddy who was walking behind. 'This dude is crazy, thinking *he* can talk to me like that.'

Both of them began to laugh. I knew that they knew that I was a girl; they were just being petty, which only made me angrier.

'Yeah you're real funny,' I said sarcastic-ally, throwing my books to the floor and lunging after him. Before he could know what was happening, I'd punched him in the face, and hard.

He fell back towards the wall, and then tried to come towards me. His friend was watching, stunned. The next few moments passed quickly. I remember grabbing his shirt, ripping it and trying to hit him a few more times. He was in the school wrestling team however, so before I knew it he had me in a headlock.

Two faculty members came running down the hallway to end the fight. One of the teachers grabbed me by the arm and pulled me aside and within a couple minutes I was in the Head's office, telling her what had happened. Needless to say, I was given a week of out-of-school suspension.

Up until the last three or four weeks of school I received many detentions and one other out-of-school suspension. I did little to no homework or class work and my grades were horrendous. I was very close to failing three out of my seven classes, which also didn't make my relationship with my mother any better.

I could tell that she was upset with me and with my grades every time she talked to me or even looked at me. Her eyes couldn't hide her pain and worry. I knew she expected more from me and was disappointed in me. Quite often she was at a loss for words. She didn't know how to help me get my life back on track, or even where to begin. She could only try to help me in her own way, which I am now thankful for, even if I didn't appreciate that at the time.

CHAPTER 9

A month before my tenth grade year was over, my mother called Ms Summerfield, the guidance counsellor. I understand why she did it now, and I'm grateful that she did. But at the time I was infuriated that she'd barged into my life like that. As I've mentioned before, I was becoming an incredibly angry and all round unhappy person; my grades were horrible and I skipped school quite a few times as well. I wouldn't talk to my own mother, so maybe an outsider would be able to reach me, right?

Funnily enough, I'd begun to notice Ms Summerfield. The way she carried herself was something I admired from afar. She seemed to be a strong and compassionate woman, not to mention absolutely gorgeous. Her long burgundy hair was like silk and her eyes reminded me of Caribbean waters. It amazed me how great her skin and complexion looked. I knew that she was a new staff member, but I wasn't sure what her job was – until the day Mom contacted her.

When I got to school that morning I was tired, sort of depressed – and a bit moody. I made sure to mind my own business. Distancing myself from everyone around me had become a normal thing, even if I didn't quite realise I was doing it. During my second class, I already wanted to leave the school building. I was bored. But I didn't leave; I just got a toilet pass from my teacher and wandered around the hallway. That way, I could be alone and rarely bothered by anyone.

After 10 minutes or so, I decided to go to the girl's toilet. I didn't need to use it, but made a habit of hiding away and smoking a cigarette. Yes, smoking is a bad habit, but it relaxed me, and cigarettes weren't hard to come by. I was never caught, so neither my mother nor Kara knew that I smoked. I just made sure I carried body spray with me in my bag, which was good for a cover-up.

In the toilet, I went to the furthest stall and stood on the seat. Hunching over wasn't always the most comfortable thing, but forgetting to be uncomfortable was easy to do. I took a cigarette out of my bag and lit it. The first inhale of smoke filled my lungs. I exhaled slowly. Making Cheerio-shaped rings with smoke was something I loved to do. They never lasted though, because I had to fan the smoke with my hands in order to reduce the smoke smell – so I thought.

When the cigarette was smoked down to its butt, I flushed it down the toilet and my smell-good-again ritual began. I would wash my hands twice, and then spray my entire body with the vanilla scented body spray taken from my mother. After smoking in a confined space you really do smell horrible; quite disgusting actually.

When I walked out of the toilet that day I thought I was in the clear. Only three or four steps away from the toilet doors, I was stopped by my history teacher, Mr Painter.

'Hiya Constance, where are you headed?' he asked me as he stood by the toilet door.

'Uhh, back to class,' I replied nonchalantly.

He stood there for a moment, taking a whiff of the stench that was still coming from the girl's toilet. I began to walk away from him, acting the complete innocent.

'Were you smoking in the toilet?'

'No. I don't smoke.'

'You smell like you do, Constance,' he said.

'Nope. I think that some girl *has* been in there smoking though,' I replied, continuing to walk back towards my classroom.

'Stop,' he said, 'I've been outside this toilet for quite a few minutes and saw only you enter and exit, so I know that *you* were the one smoking.'

I stopped in my tracks, worried and irritated, knowing that being caught smoking is a bad thing, bringing lots of trouble – from both the school *and* my mother.

'Come with me, I have to take you to the front office.'

I spent so much time in that office that I should have been on the payroll for organising flyers and hand-outs. I knew that my mother was going to be called and that I most likely was going to be suspended again; or expelled, even. Suspension was okay because it gave me a break, but being expelled? That I definitely *didn't* want.

Once I was in the front office, my mother was called. The Head spoke with her for what felt like an hour, yet was probably more like 10 minutes. What they talked about was beyond me, but I didn't like the feeling I had inside. After the phone call, the Head came out and sat next to me. We sat in silence for a few moments.

'You are lucky young lady,' he eventually said. 'Smoking on school property normally calls for an expulsion from school, which I am sure you are aware of, correct?'

I nodded my head, not saying a word.

'But after talking to your mother, I've decided to let it slide – this time. Okay?'

'Yes,' I replied.

'Under one circumstance, however.'

Not liking the sound of that, I began to have an unsettling feeling in the pit of my stomach. This could be huge, then again it could be something stupid.

'We have a new counsellor in school, Ms Summerfield. Do you know who she is?' he asked.

'I've seen her around.'

'Well, she is part of a programme dealing with troubled kids. Not that you are troubled, but this would be a way for you to get your grades up to par and avoid being expelled. Your mother read about this new programme in the flyers we mail to the parents and this was her idea. I think it will benefit you greatly. She'll be speaking to Ms Summerfield right now, while I'm talking with you.'

It sounded stupid to me, but I was sure I could avoid talking to that woman. Why would I *want* to talk to her?

'I am going to speak with Ms Summerfield and let her know you are going to be entering her programme, which will last for the remainder of this year and into next year, okay?'

'Sure,' I said, but with a slightly sarcastic tone.

'Ms Summerfield will have you one-on-one, the last class period of the day. Sometimes she might pull you out of your other classes briefly to speak with you and see how your day is going. But if you mess this up, Constance, you are out. Understood?'

I was not happy about the programme at all, but I didn't have a choice in the matter. If I wanted to stay in school, I *had* to agree to it.

'Sure,' I said finally.

I was shocked that my mother had asked the Head about the programme and requested that I be placed on it. Although she saved me from expulsion, I was still quite irritated with her for interfering with my life.

Sitting in the front office for the 30 minutes until Ms Summerfield walked in was agonising. Questions about what was to come played through my mind. I didn't want her to ask me tons of questions about my life. Well, I didn't want her to ask me any questions at all for that matter, but I knew that that wouldn't happen. So I planned on avoiding any personal questions and sticking to subjects that dealt with school and grades.

When she came through the doors she walked immediately over to me, without the Head needing to introduce us. I had no idea how she knew who I was or what I looked like, but somehow she did.

'Hi Constance, I'm Ms Summerfield,' she said as she held out her hand for me to shake. 'It's nice to meet you.'

I forced a smile as we shook hands.

'Hey.'

I noticed that her hands were soft and smooth. Up close and personal, I realised that she was only in her late-twenties. Her face was wrinkle-free and glowing.

'Why don't you come with me to my office for a few minutes so that we can talk about the programme and other things, okay?' She had a soft, welcoming smile. 'I promise it won't take long. And before you know it, you will be heading home for the day.'

I nodded my head and stood up slowly.

The walk to her office wasn't far and we didn't really speak to one another on the way either. For some reason I was nervous, my stomach in knots.

Ms Summerfield's office was small but colourful, which made it seem happy. Pinned up on the wall were pictures finally from students I guessed finally along with thank-you cards and such. Her desk sat cornered to the wall, with two comfy chairs in front of it.

'Go ahead, sit down. I just have to grab a few things,' she said.

She dug around her filing cabinet for a couple of minutes, at last sitting down at her desk with a few papers in her hand. I guess she noticed the way that I was looking nervously at those papers.

'These aren't a big deal. Just a few things for you and your mom to sign. I spoke to her earlier today, so she is expecting them.'

'Oh, okay,' I responded.

'The programme you're about to begin will help you get your grades up – if you play your part. We have a point system, which will give you an incentive to do better. Once your grades go up, you will receive a coupon for a free dinner, a movie of your choice or some other things – all your choice. Now, for the remainder of this school year, our goal is to take you further away from a failing grade. I notice you are on the line, so during this next month we will work on that, okay?'

I nodded my head. It didn't seem like a bad thing at all. I'd take free pizza anytime.

'But there are a few other things we have to work on, other issues that need to be brought up as well. Your mother tells me that you have been fighting quite often and seem angry. We will also have to talk about things that are bothering you.'

'Great,' I said, becoming a little bit irritated. Why did everyone need to bug me about my life? I could figure it out on my own.

'It won't be a bad thing, I promise, and when we talk, if there is something that you are not ready to speak about that will be fine. We have the rest of the school year, the summer and the following school year to get into the aspects of your life that are bothering you.'

'The summer? What?'

'Yes. Your mother asked me if I could meet with you once a week during the summer break. I have an office in town where you can come and visit.'

Before I could stop myself, I felt my eyes roll. Why the hell had Mom asked her to do that? I wasn't crazy or anything, and I didn't need therapy!

'You don't like that idea, huh?' Ms Summerfield asked with a smile.

'Not really,' I said. 'I don't see the point of it.'

'I am here to help you, not to become an enemy.'

I sat there in silence as she spoke to me about the schedule for the rest of the school year. I listened to most of what she was saying, but for some of it I just tuned out. My mind drifted to Kara and what she was going to say about the whole ordeal. Knowing her, she would probably think it was a good idea. She was worried about me too.

Kara and I still talked everyday, but we weren't hanging out together as much as we had done. This was mostly because of my own issues and the feelings I had for her. And I didn't want to reveal them, afraid that she would think I was nuts. Still, I knew that one day that would happen, unless I could keep my emotions from going wild every time she was in sight. I liked how I felt, but I was also scared.

By the end of the school year, my grades were still not the greatest, but I didn't fail any of my classes. Ms Summerfield and I didn't talk much about my personal life during those few weeks, but I knew that it was coming. The summer break was going to be the worst I'd ever had, and I hated thinking about what was going to happen. What was she going to ask me? From my perspective, an hour with her once a week was going to be a waste of time. It turned out, though, not to be a waste of time at all.

CHAPTER 10

High school is normally a time when you meet great friends and go to school dances, not to mention the tons of school functions that students attend year-round. It is also a time when a teenager truly finds themself and perhaps what they would like to do in the future. In my case the majority of my high school days were hellish, not because of anyone else, but because of me really. I look back at the last couple years and wonder how or why they flew by so quickly. I guess I don't regret anything though; I've only gained knowledge and strength.

Today as I enter the school I remember the past and why it is just that – the past.

Holding onto hardships will not make life any easier and this year, my senior year, is going to be different. I can feel it.

Kara and I walk through the entrance doors of the school giggling at something ridiculous. She has a certain facial expression that makes me laugh every time she does it, no matter what. I guess she senses that I am a little tense, and a bit of laughter always helps.

'You're crazy, Kara,' I say while laughing, almost hysterically. 'That gets me every time and I must say it's such an attractive face!'

'Yeah, yeah, yeah – but 'cha love it!' she says, while giving me a quick wink.

The beginning of a normal school day is often crazed. Students hustle around searching for their first period class, while laughing and talking to each other. It always is quite obvious which kids are new to the school as well. Whether it is the student's first year in high school or if they are newcomers who transferred in, it doesn't matter, the expression on their face almost always reveals a slight panic. Finding your class in time can be a little stressful, especially in a large school that you aren't familiar with. No one wants to be late on their first day.

What I notice first are the students in the hallway. In past years I would be uptight right away, dreading the day that was to come. Today it is different. A weight has been lifted from my shoulders and I am at ease. I walk down the hall with Kara by my side and I am genuinely happy. As we make our way to our first class we pass the counsellor's office.

'Oh! Wait a minute Kara. Is it okay if I pop into Ms Summerfield's office for a minute?'

'Sure thing. I'll wait out here for ya,' she responds.

'You can come in with me if you want. I'll only be a sec.'

'It's okay. You go,' she says to me with a smile.

I nod, and then walk into the office. It looks the same as it did the year before, with hung art work, cards and a touch of sunshine. Whatever perfume Ms Summerfield wears has become my favorite; the scent fills the air and it is very soothing.

As the door closes behind me, Ms Summerfield looks up from the scattered papers that lie across her desk.

'Hey Constance! How are you?' she says, rising from her chair and walking towards me. 'It's so good to see you.'

'I'm good,' I say.

'I see you've made it for class in time.'

'Yep,' I reply with a smile, 'I'm actually excited about this year.'

'That's great!'

'It will be different, that's for sure,' I say with a smirk.

'I'm glad you stopped by, I was wondering how you were. It's been a while. How was your summer?'

'Nice. I just stayed around the house mostly with some friends.'

'Wonderful,' she says with her catching smile, her eyes glowing.

'Well, I guess I should get to class. I just wanted to say 'hi'.'

'I'm glad you did. Stop in any time, okay? And if you need anything, I'm here... you know that right?'

'Yep,' I reply, while nodding.

Somehow after leaving Ms Summerfield's office, I feel better than I did a few moments ago. Frequently she has that capability, to make everything seem much more positive. I am glad.

Kara is leaning up against the wall outside the office. Well, hunching over, actually.

'What are you doing?' I yell over to her.

'Trying to find my damn timetable, I don't know where it is,' she says, while practically ripping apart her bag. 'Where is yours?'

'Right here.'

I open the front part of my bag and reveal my timetable. Kara looks up, but continues to dig around for her own. She turns around and places her bag on the ground. The funny thing is, as she does this I notice something white hanging out of the single pocket on her skirt.

'Uh. Have you checked your pocket?'

'What pocket? I don't have any.'

Her eyes follow my finger, as I point to the timetable that is falling out of the oddly placed pocket. She pulls the timetable out and looks at it in disbelief.

'Oh my, I'm losing it,' she says.

She smacks her forehead jokingly and starts to laugh.

Kara and I walk down the hall towards our first class, the only class we have together this year. However, we are both on work study which means after our fifth period class, halfway through our day, we are able to leave the premises. It is a great opportunity because we can choose either an internship or a regular job to give us work experience before we graduate.

It's amazing that in a span of only a year my life has changed almost completely. A revelation about life can hit you like a ton of bricks if it is at the right time, and I guess I was ready. Ready for a promising life and future.

The summer between my tenth and eleventh grade year was when the shifting began. It happened slowly, but at least it happened.

The duration of summer break is about three months, and for a month of that I stayed in hibernation. My room became a place where I hid from the outside world, only throwing myself back into reality when I was hungry. I didn't talk to my mom, avoided Kara and made up every excuse possible to stay away from a therapy session with Ms Summerfield. In the first month I only saw her once and not one peep came out of my mouth. I refused to talk to her.

When the second month was approaching, my mother decided to take control of the situation and practically force me to see Ms Summerfield. It took her three hours of fighting with me until I gave in.

Ms Summerfield's office was in town, five miles away from our house. I tried to convince my mother to let me walk, but she knew better – I wouldn't have actually gone. Anyway, the drive to her office was miserable. I was angry with my mother, forcing me to do something I had no desire to do.

My mother and I argued the entire way and at one point I almost jumped out of the car – not when it was moving of course. We came to a red stop light and I decided to open the door and get out. I didn't make it. Our car turned abruptly, avoiding traffic and went down another road. At the time I swore my mom had gone crazy. What was she trying to do, seriously injure me? Not really, she'd just lost all tolerance and wasn't taking any more attitude from me. Which is good, I guess – now.

Once we made it safely to Ms Summerfield's, Mother walked me in. She didn't trust me enough to drop me off outside of the building, like she did the previous time.

Talking about my inner feelings, my fears, weaknesses and doubts was very hard for me. The thought of it made my skin crawl. I didn't want anyone to think I was crazy or weird and if anyone truly knew, they would think I was wacko for sure.

I sat in a huge, comfy blue couch in front of Ms Summerfield, who sat in a chair like a sort of recliner. My session was supposed to be only an hour long, so I figured if I looked at my feet long enough, it would be over quite quickly. I didn't want to make eye contact either, because I knew it would start a conversation – but I did glance at her for a moment. She was so beautiful.

'There you are, Constance. I finally see your beautiful eyes,' she said in a soft voice.

My face began to feel hot, like it was on fire. I tried to shove back the smile that was surfacing, but it didn't work. In that instant, she mildly had my attention – and she knew it.

'I think this is the first time you've looked away from the floor since you've been coming to see me. That's a start,' she said, with a smile.

Before I knew it, she and I were having more of a real conversation. I still felt anxious, but it wasn't as extreme. The way she spoke to me was in a friendly manner, not in a clinical way at all, making the conversation easier. I felt like she cared and was truly interested in my life.

'Believe it or not, I understand how it feels to be on the outside looking in, Constance. I spent a majority of my childhood possibly feeling like you do now, and I want to help you – if you let me,' she said to me.

'You couldn't possibly understand how it feels to be me. There's no way.'

Ms. Summerfield moved her chair closer to me, making me a tad nervous. I knew she was trying to reach out to me, but there was no way she understood how I felt.

'Try me.'

'What do you want me to say? I don't know!'

'I know it's frustrating to talk about feelings or emotions, but say whatever you feel – even if it's anger,' she advised me. 'What angers you the most?'

'I don't like to be picked on, looked down on or made fun of, and when people do – I get angry.' I felt the adrenaline beginning to stew within, even talking about such matters got to me. 'I know I'm different, probably not that attractive, but people call me horrible things... so, I decided to take care of it myself, and not deal with it.'

'First off Constance, you are unique, but that is what makes you – you. You have your own great style, likes, dislikes and hobbies. There is not another you in this world and that makes you so special,' she said with an intent gaze. 'You are a beautiful young lady.'

I remember thinking, 'Beautiful? Are you crazy?' I wasn't used to hearing that from anyone except my mother – and it was her job to tell me that, even if I looked like a hyena. Kara told me I was 'cute' quite a few times though, but I didn't know what that meant, or how to take it.

The remainder of my session with Ms Summerfield that day went well, considering it was the first time I opened up. Don't get me wrong, I was inhibited, but not as much as I was when we first started. Making a change starts with baby steps — until we are ready to leap.

I met Ms Summerfield in her office every Wednesday for the next two months. Expressing my thoughts became much easier and we were actually getting somewhere. We focused on my anger and self-esteem issues, and briefly discussed how I felt at home. I didn't talk about my hidden issues though, the fact that I might be gay, for fear of a bad reaction. I had a need to keep those thoughts to myself until I figured them out.

A few of our sessions were interrupted by crying spells. I'd find myself mentioning how ashamed I was and how pathetic I felt, which caused the tears. I was hurting, but talking about it actually made me feel better — even a bit stronger.

Ms Summerfield offered a good amount of information about herself. She told me that she grew up with her mother and that her father left when she was only two years old. She had to get a job at a young age to help her mother pay rent and often she was bullied in school because of her clothes. They were old, tatty and torn, and because of that she became an outcast, just like I was. She really did understand where I was coming from.

Often my sessions were immediately after lunch and quite a few times she was having lunch with her roommate Jo-Ann when I arrived. Jo-Ann and Ms Summerfield were not just roommates but best friends as well. They did everything together, just like Kara and I did. But I could tell they were more than just friends by the way they looked at each other. It was none of my business really, yet I had a notion that Ms Summerfield and I had even more in common than we thought.

CHAPTER 11

It is always interesting when a class has reached its capacity. The combination of above average, average and below average students often acts like a chemical reaction. Those who study constantly and have panic attacks over a 'C' on an exam paper don't get along well with students who are disruptive and don't have a care in the world. When a teacher is able to contain the classroom, all is well – but if the teacher is new and doesn't have a clue, the class becomes a playground that breeds madness.

As Kara and I walk into our first class we notice that it is going to be a difficult one. Our teacher Mrs Peters must be new, because she is sitting behind her desk frantically looking through the register. The room is noisy, already bringing annoyance to a select few in the room. I look at Kara with a half-smile and motion over to the two vacant desks in the corner.

'This shall be fun,' I mumble sarcastically.

I sit in the seat next to Kara, looking around the room silently. It's insane. I don't recognise anyone either, which is odd. No one paid any attention to Kara and me as we walked into the room - or the teacher who seems to be stiff as a board, still hiding behind her desk. Most of the students seem to be groups of friends because they are huddling together, discussing their exciting and fantastic summer. Boy, I wish they would shut up!

Through the crowded classroom I notice a familiar face sitting in the far corner of the room. Sean is paging through his notebook, obviously trying to ignore the noise. He has never been one to handle noise and crowds very well, although he is getting better. I tap Kara on the shoulder and discreetly point over in Sean's direction. The feeling of someone watching him must have grabbed hold of him because he immediately looks up and in our direction. He politely smiles and acknowledges us.

The relationship Sean and I have is probably a little odd for the views of some. We aren't the best of friends, but at the same time we are more than just friendly acquaintances. He, Kara and I still hang out together sometimes. We get together for a movie, lunch or meet at the local coffee house every once in a while. Amazingly enough, there are no hard feelings between him and me. He is very understanding and cool when it comes to my situation.

It wasn't always like that though. We didn't speak to one another for about two years – until the middle of our eleventh grade year. Before that we would occasionally say 'hello' to each other while we passed in the halls, but not too often. I am glad to have him back in my life.

My eleventh grade year was a time to get myself together and grow as a person. I didn't intend for it to turn out that way, it just happened.

Once I returned to classes that year, things began to change pretty abruptly. Routinely, because of the year before, I still didn't talk to many other students. Frankly, I avoided any confrontation. During the summer Ms Summerfield and I dealt with my anger issues a little, but I didn't trust myself completely yet. At that point, I wasn't sure if I had the strength to hold back my anger if someone were to joke or make a comment about me.

Within the first month of classes I quickly became the same person I was the year before. I was sent to the office a few times for fighting and even suspended for a couple days. Ms Summerfield pulled me out of my classes at least three times a day to speak with me. She would ask me how I was feeling and if I wanted to talk about anything. Often she questioned me, asking me why I was falling back into the same black hole I was stuck in the year before. I was at a loss for words, unable to give her an answer. The truth was, I didn't know why I was letting myself fall back into all of the negativity. I surely didn't want to be that way, but before I knew what came over me, I would lose my cool.

Some days were worse than others. I'd want to hide from everyone, and I did. I would leave my classroom and go to the girl's bathroom, not to smoke – I had quit – but to get away. I would crawl into a stall and stay there for most of my class period. My mind would race, trying to solve the questions that continuously reentered my thoughts. I ached so deeply and at times would cry until I couldn't produce any more tears.

Maybe Ms Summerfield could talk to someone to prescribe me medication, I'd think. I was past the point of thinking I was sane. Something had to be wrong with me to cry on a whim, become enraged in a split second and to have the thoughts I did about girls. Why me? I'd ask myself over and over again. Woe is me, I know – but that is what went through my mind.

The only plus side of things at that time was the fact that my grades were the highest they had been for a couple years. My lack of enthusiasm in the classroom was an everyday occurrence, but once at home I'd bury myself into my studies. I found history to be especially interesting. To learn about hardships in distant countries intrigued me, especially when the people were able to rise above their difficulties. In a sense, it gave me hope.

For the first few months of that year, Kara and I spent little time together. We would talk to each other in school and on the phone every night, but rarely met after school or on weekends. She would ask me to do things with her, but I couldn't bear the thought. Spending time with her became almost overwhelmingly difficult. I found myself getting lost in her words or eyes and had a hard time snapping out of it, which scared me. Being obvious about my feelings was something I didn't want. And I knew if I kept on having that reaction when

I was around her – the emotions I felt *would* be known.

The first day of my self-realisation is one I will never forget; it feels like only yesterday. It was a Thursday evening, quite dreary and brisk outside. The majority of the day was great, I was in a good mood and actually happy. I felt good – good enough to sit down and spend time with my mother, something I hardly ever did.

We had seafood that night for dinner, such a treat. Mother got a payrise at work so she wanted to celebrate with her favourite food. It was my favourite as well. The table was covered with crab legs and steamed shrimp and I remember eating way too much. But I was happy with that. Once in a while pigging out isn't so bad. Anyway, let me get back to what I was saying.

After dinner I helped mother clean the kitchen, and then went into the living room with her to watch some television. At first we didn't talk much, just watched a comedy show, which caused my mom to laugh so hard she blew tea out of her mouth. It was a hilarious sight, which caused contagious laughing spells for a few minutes. After she and I calmed down, an unexpected conversation began. I was okay with the topic for a minute or so, until it changed abruptly.

'That was fun... laughing with you,' mother said to me, with a hint of amusement in her voice.

'Yeah it was. It's been a while.'

'That's for sure,' she replied. 'How was school today?'

'It was okay I guess. Same stuff, ya know?' I said, turning my head to look at her.

'You know you can talk to me about anything, right Constance?'

That question alone made me a tad nervous. It didn't sound good to me at all and I wasn't sure I liked where the conversation was headed. But, I decided to respond to her anyway.

'Sure I do. Why are you asking?'

'Oh, I don't know. I just wanted to make sure that you know that I am always here if you need to talk about anything.'

'What would I need to talk about? I tell you some things,' I said, suddenly feeling myself become anxious.

'Can I ask you something?'

'Depends on what it is. But, yeah.'

'I don't want this to come out the wrong way and I apologise if it does, but are you gay?'

Immediately I became defensive, more than was needed. I couldn't believe she had asked me that and I didn't like it one bit!

'What? Are you kidding? Why would you ask me a question like that?' I said with a louder than normal voice.

'I just want you to know that it's okay if you are and I am here for you.'

'You've gone mad! What is your problem? What gives you that crazy idea? That's gross, Mom!' I yelled. 'What, just because I don't do cheerleading or wear dresses, I'm gay? And maybe I just don't want a boyfriend right now, did you ever think of that? Plenty of guys at school want to go out with me, but I say no.'

'Calm down honey, it's okay. I just wanted to ask, and tell you that if you are, it's fine. It is quite a common thing nowadays; I've read up on it.'

'You've what?' I screamed. 'Crazy! You know what? Maybe you are the queer one, Mom; you haven't had a man in your life for years! Maybe that's why you read up on it and you are ashamed and trying to make me the one who's a homo! That, I am not!' I screamed, while standing up away from the couch.

'Alright, alright calm down. Let's watch some more TV and forget I ever asked.'

'Forget that you asked? No way! You practically accused me! Are you that ashamed to have me as your daughter?' I said, tears falling from my eyes.

'No, no. God, I'm sorry sweetie,' she said softly while reaching her hands out to me.

'Don't touch me! I don't want to be near you right now!' And with that comment, I left.

I didn't just leave the living room, but left the house as well. Outside rain began to fall and I was barefoot. I walked along the street for hours, drenched, freezing and infuriated. Yet, at the same time I was incredibly sad and worried. Why did she ask me that question? Were my inner feelings visible for the world to see? Was I gay? No way, there was no way! I mean, it was normal for some girls not to have boyfriends throughout high school – and be a tomboy, right? I knew plenty of girls in school who were tomboys, playing sports and who never wore dresses. Some of them did have boyfriends though. Maybe I was like those girls, minus the boyfriend?

I didn't return home that night until after midnight. When I walked through the front door I noticed that Mother was sleeping on the couch, probably trying to wait up for me. However, she didn't budge as I walked past the living room and up the steps to my bedroom.

The beginning of that day was almost perfect, yet it ended miserably. I was depressed and wanted to go to sleep for days. I dreaded waking up the next morning weary and tired, and seeing my mom. I wasn't ready to talk to her at that point about anything. But maybe a good night's sleep, or at least the good five hours I had left to sleep, would help clear my mind.

I knew one thing was for sure though – once I was in school the next day, I was going to tell Ms Summerfield about everything that had happened. I wondered what she would think about it, or what she would say. I wasn't sure how I was going to bring it up, but I didn't really care. I would figure that out when the time came. I just needed to talk to her, and fast.

CHAPTER 12

My alarm ringing in my ear the following morning was the last thing I wanted to hear. I didn't sleep a wink; my mind wandered all night – so much it almost drove me crazy. My body was craving sleep, yet my mind didn't want it. Still, I pulled myself out of bed anyway, only because I wanted to get into school and talk with Ms. Summerfield. Otherwise I would have faked being sick.

Before leaving my house that morning I ate breakfast in silence, steering clear of any contact with my mother. A few times she tried to apologise for the night before, but I ignored every word she spoke to me.

Once I finished eating, I grabbed my bag and ran out of the house. I felt so strange, my mind and body still being affected by the argument. My anxiety level was extremely high and I couldn't imagine sitting in class, knowing I'd be fidgety. So I decided to skip first period.

I ran into Ms Summerfield's office first thing. Speaking with her right away as I had planned didn't happen because there was another student talking with her already. I sat in a chair outside her office while I waited – which felt like forever. By the time I was able to talk with her all of my fingernails were gone.

She greeted me with a gentle smile, immediately aware something was wrong.

'Are you okay, Constance?' she asked.

'Uhh, I guess so.'

'You don't look it. Why don't you sit down?'

I sat down in a chair in front of her desk, but instead of her sitting behind the desk like usual, she pulled a chair up next to mine.

'Is there something on your mind? You look upset,' she questioned.

'My mom and I got in a huge fight last night and she really pissed me off. Sometimes I think she is crazy!'

'What happened?'

'The night started out good and I was actually in an okay mood, so I decided to watch some TV with her. We never do that, ya know? And now I know why! She's nuts!' I began. 'Anyway, we were laughing at a show that was on, and then she messed it up! Out of nowhere she asked me if I were gay!'

'And that made you angry?' she asked me politely.

'Of course it did! I think she only asked me that because *she* has tendencies or she is just ashamed of me and wanted to make up a reason to make me more of a screw up than I already am.'

'You are *not* a screw up, not at all! Look how far you have come.'

'Well, why would she ask me that? I mean, I knew that my mom thinks I am weird, she has for years, but that's a disgusting thing for her to ask! A girl being with another girl is gross and something I could never do! She just hates who I am!'

'Do you really think it is gross, Constance? Or are you just afraid of anyone else who is different than you?'

'I'm not afraid of people who are different, but it doesn't make any sense to me. Am I *supposed* to have a boyfriend? And if I don't, am I automatically a queer or a fairy?'

'I understand how you are feeling, I've been there.'

'How have you been here before? I mean, no one could have ever called you a queer – you look normal.'

'Let me ask you this. Do you really think that being gay is weird or gross?'

'Yeah!' I responded, with no hesitation.

Ms Summerfield sat there for a moment simply looking at me. I knew she was thinking about something, but wasn't sure what. I hoped that I didn't offend her or anything. Things just flew out of my mouth before I could shove them back in because I was so worked up.

'Do you think I'm gross?'

'What?' I asked, completely surprised with her question. 'No way! You're a cool person.'

'Well then Constance, you should not judge anyone, no matter what. I am a lesbian.'

When she told me that I froze in my seat and felt horrible for saying the things I did.

I had a feeling that she might have been, but wasn't sure – until then. The thought probably wouldn't have ever crossed my mind if I hadn't met her roommate during the summer. The only thing that gave me a clue was their relationship – it seemed so much closer than the norm. For a few minutes I didn't say a word. A lump formed in my throat and I felt tears filling my eyes. I didn't want to cry. Why would I cry?

'And the fact that I am gay doesn't make me different than anyone else,' she continued, 'I have goals, wants and needs, just like everyone else in the world – including love. So what if I fell in love with a woman? I am who I am.'

I knew that she was telling me all of this, so I would feel better inside. She probably already knew that I was gay, but wasn't going to approach the matter in the way my mother did.

'Have you ever been made fun of because of that?' I asked her, not knowing where the question came from. I hoped that I wasn't asking *too* much, but she replied quickly.

'Yes a few times, but nothing huge or anything. Some people are just close-minded and don't understand or even try to understand. They fear what is different, so they assume making fun of it is the answer. I've learned to ignore it pretty easily.'

I couldn't stop them before they fell, tears streaming down my face. I was embarrassed to be crying as hard as I was and for no reason, but they continued to fall.

'I-I'm sorry,' I stuttered, in between my almost loud cry.

'Sorry for what? It's okay. I told you that you can talk to me about anything,' she said in a soft voice, and reached out and gave my arm a gentle squeeze.

I felt like a baby, stupid for crying, but she made me feel better.

Missing both my first and second period class wasn't a big deal; Ms Summerfield filled out an excuse slip for me. She and I didn't talk that entire time, I just wasn't able to gather myself together quickly enough. Going into a classroom with red eyes and out of sorts was not something I aimed to do – I would get too much negative attention from others.

While in her office, I spent the majority of the time looking out of the window, watching the rain pound against the cars in the parking lot. I wasn't that interested in rain but it was soothing, and took my mind to a distant place. It wasn't too far from reality, but distant enough that I began to feel at ease.

My thoughts were somewhat odd, yet didn't disturb me. My first thoughts were about Kara, her smile, laugh and tenderness. She was the most caring person I knew – well, besides Ms Summerfield. No matter what I was going through she was always there for me. She loved me, as a friend. I knew I loved her, cared about her and never wanted our friendship to end. I wasn't sure what I'd do if she weren't in my life anymore.

I began to draw on an imaginary canvas in my mind as well. I drew Kara and me next to each other in a meadow, joking around as usual, having a picnic with ham sandwiches, chips and iced tea. I quickly snapped out of it when I realised she and I were around thirty years old in the daydream. Weird.

'What the hell was that?' I whispered quietly to myself.

It was in that brief second when a rush of realisation fell upon me. I didn't accept it fully, but was ten steps closer to the truth, more than I was just two days before. Thoughts rushed in, surprisingly enough, not overwhelming me completely. *Am I in love with Kara and have I been this entire time? How can that be? What will I do if I am really gay? I want a normal life, to be successful and maybe one day have a family – could I still do that? What do I do? Please, someone please tell me what to do!*

Tears began to fall, yet unlike any other time before I felt a huge release of tension that had built up inside me for so long. I didn't admit it to myself completely, but the thought of the possibility was surfacing quickly.

After that day, the rest of my eleventh grade school year went swiftly. My grades were above average and I didn't get into any more fights or receive detentions. Talking with Ms Summerfield that day must have helped me become a little stronger, making it much easier to ignore comments made to me by other people. After all if she could proudly be herself no matter what sort of ridicule she experienced, I should be able to brush off bullies and their nasty remarks, right? I even started to spend more time with Kara again and talked to more kids in school as well.

One day towards the end of the school year, Kara and I were in the library looking for a specific book for our research project. We spent at least an hour searching for it by ourselves before confronting the librarian to help. Kara was the one speaking to her, which gave me time to look around, paying no attention to their conversation. To my surprise, Sean was in the line that was forming behind us – smiling in my direction. So, I waved.

Sean, Kara and I began to sit together at lunch again after that day. I was glad that he didn't have any hard feelings towards me because of our break-up, and sometimes it was fun to be in his company. To have all three of us together again at lunch some days felt like old times – except he and I weren't dating, of course.

Going to school everyday without a giant weight on my shoulder felt incredible and I was happy about that. A sense of fear lingered within me, but I tried my hardest to fight it – and for the most part it worked.

I had a fear of rejection, loss and other people's opinions about me mostly. I was improving, but still wasn't able to talk about something deep or along the subject line of homosexuality either. I wasn't quite *that* comfortable with the topic, or in my own skin for that matter. I talked to myself every night about it though and started to keep a journal, hoping it would make things easier to figure out. Baby steps, remember?

Finding myself was important and I knew that it was going to happen. Change can be a good thing, no matter if it is unexpected. In my case, the changing of everything in my life wasn't as unexpected as I played it out to be. I just chose to ignore everything around me, even my inner thoughts and feelings. But the time came when I was *ready*.